Kat
Karnival

City Limits

Hank's
House →

CATSBURG

How the GHERKINS STOLE CHRISTMAS

Curiosity Books
An imprint of Curiosity Ink Media, LLC
15301 Ventura Boulevard, Building B, Suite 340
Sherman Oaks, CA 91403
www.curiosityinkmedia.com

How the Gherkins Stole Christmas

Correspondence regarding the content of this book should be sent to Curiosity Books, Editorial Department, at the above address.

ISBN: 978-1-948206-68-6

Printed in China

1 3 5 7 9 10 8 6 4 2

How the GHERKINS STOLE CHRISTMAS

WRITTEN BY
D.M. FARRELL

ILLUSTRATED BY
GABRIELE TAFUNI

CURIOSITY BOOKS   Ink Media   LOS ANGELES

Ah, Christmas in Catsburg.

A lovely time of year to cherish friendship,
celebrate family, appreciate the unique sights,
sounds, smells, and . . .

Say, this isn't what Catsburg is supposed to be like at Christmas!
Why, these cats aren't in the holiday spirit AT ALL!

Where is the connection? Where is the kindness? Where is the love?
If these cats can't get in the loving spirit at Christmas, well . . .
the rest of this year could be pretty sad indeed.

Hey, you pickles look like Santa's little green elves! Maybe you can do something about all the bah humbugs going around!

Will you devise an ingenious plan? Yes? Oh, I knew you'd come through!

The pickles are going to save Christmas in Catsburg!

What's this?

Wow! You pickles have REALLY outdone yourselves! Your very own sleigh!

Now you can get around in style, just like Santa does! You pickles sure are smart!

Whoa! Pickle reindeer! Those must be magical antlers!

I can't wait to see this sleigh sailing through the night sky!
Oh. That's not what I had in mind. But it's still GENIUS!

You pickles are the best!
I hope this plan works in time!!

Evening, Snowball!

Well, you're certainly in the Christmas spirit!
You sure do look happy!

What is the deal with the other cats in Catsburg?
I don't think they've caught the holiday spirit yet.

Do you?

Don't worry, Snowball. I've got a sneaky
feeling the Christmas spirit will be returning
to Catsburg . . . any . . . minute . . . now . . . .

Snowball! Did you see that?

Why! I think it might be . . .

ALIENS?

Aliens?

I don't know, Snowball.

Maybe we should follow that unidentified flying object and see what it's up to. You might be surprised.

Go, Snowball! You're hot on the trail!!

I think if you creep a little bit closer,
you'll see that the green glow belongs to an . . .

No! Don't you recognize those little silhouettes, Snowball?
Don't they look a little bit like . . .

Snowball, I'm glad you made it home safely.

wait . . . What was that?

Snowball, are you seeing what I'm seeing? O.M.G . . . Go get 'em, Snowball!

Oh, Snowball, I hope you catch whoever's doing this!

Just around this corner . . .

I bet you'll find . . . the . . .

No, not aliens!

Snowball, come back!

wait!
Snowball, don't do it.

Oh, Snowball, this won't end well.

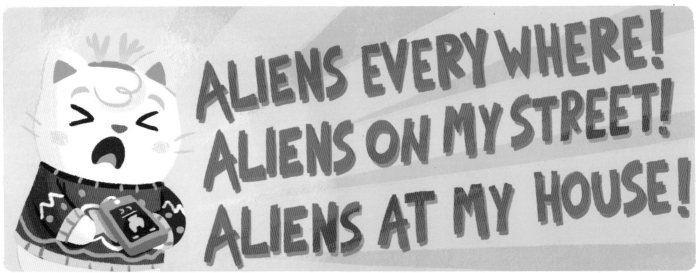

Pickles! This is NOT how you
save Christmas in Catsburg!

I'm starting to get nervous
about your "plan."

what do you mean, don't worry?!?

Why are you pickles taking the Christmas tree?

And the candy canes?

Not the sweater!

Please, don't ruin this sweet holiday moment.

Pickles, how could you?!

This is a very bad idea. There are going
to be some very hungry cats in Catsburg!

Pickles, I'm speechless.

Snowball! What are you doing?

Please stop, Snowball. It's not what you think! Let me explain!

Don't take the wreath!

Not the mistletoe, too?

You're even taking the presents?

You can't steal EVERYTHING!

Uh-oh, Snowball, uh-oh pickles, you both may have FINALLY gone too far!

A blimp? Snowball! You're going to get in trouble.

Watch out! You're going to run into Presicat's Christmas tree!

Uh-oh, Snowball. Now you're in big, big trouble.
I did try to warn you . . .

And you, pickles! Treats? Christmas trees?
What else could you possibly take?!

Grass sledding?

Mud angels?

Oh no! What have those pickles done now?

Did you take away all the snow in Catsburg?

I can't believe
the pickles stole
Santa, too!

Catsburg is so sad!

Are you pickles trying to ruin Christmas?

You're definitely on the naughty list now!

Where's that song coming from?

Snowball, follow and find out where everyone is going.

Who could have done such a kind thing? Who has every
cat in Catsburg celebrating face to face like one big family?

It was the pickles!

Snowball was right . . . sort of.
It was little green men, after all!

SORRY...

So, pickles, what do you wish for from Santa?

Look at that! You wished for Snowball to
become the Catsburg Christmas Queen!

I love it!

I think this Christmas
will go down in Catsburg history.

PawnaLuLu
Beach

Cat PaRK